# Sea Surprise

# Sea Surprise

## LEO LANDRY

*An Early Chapter Book*

Henry Holt and Company
New York

Henry Holt and Company, LLC
*Publishers since 1866*
115 West 18th Street
New York, New York 10011
www.henryholt.com

Henry Holt is a registered trademark of Henry Holt and Company, LLC
Copyright © 2005 by Leo Landry
Distributed in Canada by H. B. Fenn and Company Ltd.

Library of Congress Cataloging-in-Publication Data
Landry, Leo.
Sea surprise / Leo Landry.—1st ed.
p.    cm.
Summary: Kate the mermaid and her undersea friends
try to help an electric eel recover his "zap."
ISBN-13: 978-0-8050-6645-6
ISBN-10: 0-8050-6645-4
[1. Electric eel—Fiction.  2. Eels—Fiction.  3. Marine animals—Fiction.
4. Friendship—Fiction.] I. Title.
PZ7.L2317357Se 2005   [Fic]—dc22    2004023391

First Edition—2005 / Designed by Patrick Collins
Printed in the United States of America on acid-free paper. ∞

1  3  5  7  9  10  8  6  4  2

*For Mary*

*With thanks to Laura Godwin
and Reka Simonsen*

# Contents

# Sea Surprise

# ~1~
# A Morning Swim

It was a cool, wet day at the bottom of the sea. Above the waves, a storm was brewing. Far below, safe from the storm, Kate and Dave were out for a morning swim along the coral reef.

"What shall we do today, Dave?" asked Kate, flipping her tail idly.

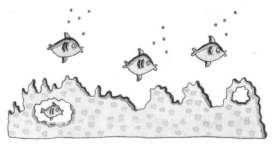

"Let's bite something," said Dave. Dave was bored, and boredom always made his teeth itch.

"No," said Kate. "Why do you always want to go around biting things?"

"It is what I do," answered Dave simply.

"Well, it is not what I do," said Kate. "Let's go and visit Eel instead. I haven't seen him since last week, and I miss his electric-eel glow."

"We could visit Eel and bite something," Dave muttered to himself.

The two friends swam off together toward Eel's house.

# ~ 2 ~
# A Sick Friend

Eel was ill. He did not wake up feeling very electric. This was not a good sign. He was an electric eel. He tried to zap on the light at his bedside with his tail. When he touched the lamp, nothing happened.

"Oh, drat!" he said grumpily. "I've lost my zap!"

He tried the lamp again but remained in the dark.

*Ding!* rang the doorbell.

"Go away!" shouted Eel.

"It is your friends, Kate and Dave," said Kate and Dave.

"I am sick. I seem to have lost my zap. The door is unlocked. Come in," said Eel.

Kate and Dave swam through the open door. They saw their good friend lying in bed. He was as pale as a sea jelly.

"What's wrong?" asked Kate. She was concerned.

"When I woke up today," Eel answered, tucking himself farther under the covers, "I felt as weak as a sea slug. As flat as a flounder. And when I tried to use my zap to turn on my light, I had no glow. No charge. No e-l-e-c-t-r-i-c-i-t-y."

"Then I will make you some sea tea," offered Kate.

"And I will give your tail a good bite," offered Dave.

"Try it, and I will zap you," said Eel. "Once I get my zap back."

"Nobody understands me," said Dave. His lower lip stuck out as he pouted. "I was only trying to help." He looked around and saw a pie on Eel's kitchen shelf.

"If you two help me get my zap back, I might let you have a bite of that plankton pie you have your eye on," said Eel.

Dave's eyes widened in delight. Plankton pie was his favorite dessert.

"It's a deal," said Dave, smiling. "Let's go, Kate. We have got work to do."

# ~3~
# The Wreck

"Where are we going?" asked Kate, as they raced along the bottom of the sea.

"To the wreck," said Dave. "I am hoping that Puff will help us."

Kate and Dave soon reached the wreck. The sunken ship had been lying on the ocean floor for many years. Its tall mast reached all the way up above the waves.

"Puff is always hiding around here. We will find her," said Dave. "Ha! There she is now."

Puff was warily peeking out from a broken teacup. She had not yet seen her friends.

"Watch this," said Dave, snickering to himself. Silently, he swam up behind the cup.

"Woo woo!" he shouted.

*Whoosh!* went Puff. She inflated like a balloon and popped out of the teacup in a nervous flutter.

"Hi, there!" said Dave with a wicked grin.

"Eek!" squeaked Puff. "You really scared me, Dave!"

"You were already scared," said Dave. "What are you hiding from?"

"There is a big storm up above," explained Puff. "I am afraid of the thunder and lightning."

"But that is way up there," said
Dave. "We are way down here."

"You never know," said Puff. She
was always very cautious.

" 'Fraidy fish," said Dave.

"Stop it, you two!" Kate snapped.
"We are wasting time. Puff, Eel is ill.
He woke up without his electric-eel
energy, and we are trying to help him
get his zap back," said Kate. "Will you
join us?"

"I g-guess so," said Puff nervously. She took a deep gulp of water. "But keep Dave away from me. He makes me jumpy."

"Don't worry," said Dave. "I will leave you alone now. It's time to help our good pal Eel feel better. And then, of course, we can have a big bite of his plankton pie."

# ~4~
# A Plan

Kate, Dave, and Puff needed a plan.
Kate thought, and twirled her tail.

Dave thought, and chewed on a fin.

Puff thought, and stuck out her spines.

"I have it!" shouted Puff. "Maybe if—"

"We bit him?" interrupted Dave.

"No!" said Puff. "No biting today! I was going to suggest something that I read in a book I found at the wreck. Maybe if he drank a glass of water without taking a breath he would get his zap back."

"That is a cure for hiccups," said Kate. "I don't think it works for zaps."

"Besides, we live in the sea," said Dave. "We breathe water."

"Oh," said Puff, deflating a bit. She thought harder.

"Hot soup?" she asked at last.

"A cure for a cold," said Kate.

"Tie a warm wool scarf around his neck?" suggested Puff.

"Sore throat," answered Kate, and sighed.

The three undersea friends looked down at the seafloor and thought once more.

"I've got it!" exclaimed Dave.

"Of course! We call a sea doctor!" shouted Puff.

"No!" Dave paused, and just managed not to bite Puff. "No, no, no. I've got a plan. Get everyone together and meet back here in one hour. It's time for a surprise party!"

# ~ 5 ~
# Eel Sets Out

Eel awoke from a long, restful nap. He had been dreaming of sneaking up on Dave and giving him a tiny little shock as he bit into the plankton pie. Eel was feeling better, and feebly tried again to turn on his reading lamp. He still did not have his zap back.

Bored and lonely, he glanced at his sea clock. Hours had passed since Kate and Dave's visit.

"My friends have forgotten all about me," he said to himself sadly. "Maybe they are at the wreck," he guessed. "Or maybe they are having a party without me."

Then he perked up. "I think I will try to find them. Maybe they have found a way to restore my zap!"

So Eel packed up his plankton pie, snuggled into his favorite hat, and set out for the wreck.

But when he arrived at the ship, he did not find Kate, Dave, or any of his other friends. They had said that they would help him. And they were gone.

Eel was alone.

He set the pie on the shelf that circled the mast of the ship and sat down.

"I knew it. They have forgotten me. Now I will never get my zap back," cried Eel.

# ~6~
## Party Time

Kate and Puff spent the next hour in their little sea village, gathering their friends. It was a busy day, and many of the ocean dwellers were out and about, getting things done.

There was Steve, delivering the daily mail. "Hi, there," he called to Kate.

Kate swam over and explained about Eel.

"I'll be there," Steve said. "I am almost finished with my route."

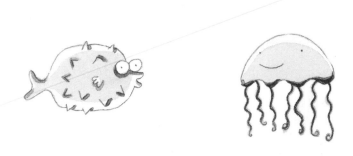

Puff saw Jill gently floating by. "Eel has lost his zap," Puff explained. "Let the others know."

"At the wreck in one hour," Kate told Ed the clam. "Eel needs our help."

Each was happy to come to a party for the ailing Eel.

Meanwhile, Dave was very busy gathering shells, bells, and anything else that made noise.

"If we make enough noise when we shout SURPRISE, the shock is sure to jolt his zap back into him!" reasoned Dave.

When an hour had passed, dozens
of Eel's undersea pals joined Kate, Puff,
and Dave at the wreck.

"Okay, Kate," said Dave. "We're here. Now it's time for you to go to Eel's house and invite him out for a swim. But don't give away the secret!"

"Just make sure you are ready when we arrive," said Kate.

"We will be," said Dave. "Puff can show us all of her best hiding places. Good luck!"

And Kate swam off toward Eel's home.

## ~7~

## Surprise!

At the wreck, wrapped around the sunken ship's mast, Eel sobbed. Through his tears, he heard a noise off in the distance. Something was coming toward the wreck.

"Whatever could that be?" he wondered.

He wiped his eyes with his tail and peered closely through the currents.

"Yikes!" he cried. "What if that is Dave's big brother? I can always tell by the look in his big shark eyes that he would like to have me for lunch! I had better hide, just to be safe."

Eel wriggled behind an old sea chest and waited for the danger to pass.

Just then Kate arrived without Eel.

"He's not home," she said to Dave sadly.

Kate, Dave, and Puff swam farther on into the wreck. There, they could see Eel's red hat peeking out from behind the chest.

"He's already here," whispered Puff, surprised. She motioned toward the sea chest with a fin. "In my favorite hiding place."

"Quick—get ready, everyone," ordered Dave to the crowd. "One, two, three . . ."

"SURPRISE!!!" they shouted. The group surrounded Eel, flapping their fins, snapping their claws, and clapping their shells. "SURPRISE!!!"

Eel leaped up in fear, shouting,
"Don't eat me! I won't shock Dave
anymore! Not even in my dreams. I
promise!"

Eel looked about and saw all of his
friends circling him, laughing and
cheering.

"Gotcha!" hollered Dave.

"Did we do it? Did we jolt your zap back into you when we yelled surprise?" asked Kate anxiously.

Eel slowly calmed down. He was relieved that he was not going to be someone's lunch today. He realized what his friends had been trying to do, and was touched. He could also tell that it had not worked. He was still without his zap.

Eel smiled. "How nice of you," he said. "I thought you had forgotten all about me. I should have known that you were all such wonderful friends. Thanks, everyone! Even if I still don't have my zap back, thank you. And have a piece of plankton pie!"

# ~ 8 ~
## At Last

"At last!" Dave cried happily. He had been waiting for this moment all day long. He opened his mouth as wide as it could go. Rows and rows of tiny little shark teeth were ready to bite into the tasty plankton pie. He swam forward eagerly.

"Wait!" cried Jill.
"Save some for us!" shouted Ed.
"We want pie!" called Steve.

CHOMP! went Dave.

"OUCH!" he cried. His teeth had gone right through the pie and into the shelf around the mast of the wrecked ship.

"Mfff," grumbled Dave. "I'm stuck! Get me OFF here!" he yelled as well as he could through his locked teeth. The friends quickly formed a chain and grabbed his tail.

PULL! went Kate, Puff, and Steve.

PULL! went Jill, Ed, and Eel.

They all pulled as hard as they could, each hanging on to the one in front.

CRACK! came the sound of thunder from above the waves.

ZAP! went a bolt of lightning as it struck the mast.

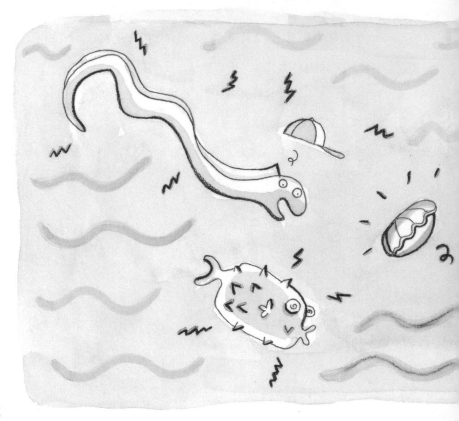

"YOW!" cried the friends. The lightning traveled down the mast, through Dave, and through the bodies of Kate, Puff, and all of the others. It stopped at last—inside Eel.

The friends were stunned. They
tingled from head to toe. Dave, now
free, counted his teeth. Eel glowed
brightly. He was his usual electric-eel
self again.

"My zap!" gasped Eel. "It's back!
You've done it!"

Everyone cheered.

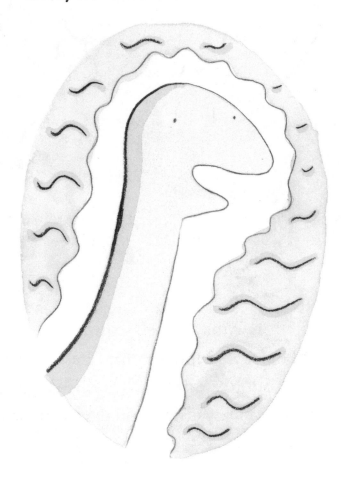

"Hooray! Hooray for Eel!" they
shouted, still tingling. And Eel gave
them each a little zap, just to say
thanks.

Kate, Puff, and the others swam Eel home, happy and safe. Eel lit the way.

And Dave took a lesson from Puff. From that day on, Dave tried to be a bit more cautious when biting.